W9-BMQ-168

Dedication

Mahalo nui loa
to Christopher Sur, Doug and Joan Warne, Shelley
Canon, and especially to Kathleen Duey, who
taught me that writing historical fiction can be
layered beyond my original vision.

Contents

Illustrations: *Page 1, 4, 6, 7, 8, 10, 16, 26, 32, 36, 43, 50, 57, 60, 68, 72, 76, 90, 102.*

Kalani and The Night Marchers

Kalani

John

Tutu

Cast of Characters

Mama

The Twins,
Eddie and Ruth

1. Are Night Marchers Real?

Kalani held the slop bucket away from his legs. "Carry it slowly," he told John. "And don't keep in step with me. We don't want it to slosh all over us."

The two boys walked a few more steps, then set the heavy bucket down to rest a moment. Kerosene lamps glowed through lace-curtained windows along the unpaved street. Mothers were calling their children in for the night.

Kalani puffed, catching his breath. His broad Hawaiian face was shiny with sweat. "I never had to do this when my real family was alive," he said. "My older brothers did all the hard stuff."

Kalani took out his handkerchief and wiped his brown forehead. He was a husky boy, half a head taller than John.

Kalani continued: "My mother wasn't as

good a storyteller as Tutu, but she was... I wish she was here."

John wiped his freckled face with his shirtsleeve. "You don't believe Tutu's stories, do you?" he asked.

Kalani blushed. "I don't know, John. The way Tutu tells them, they seem like they're true. Small-kid time, she lived by one of the paths where they say the Night Marchers go."

"What are Night Marchers?" asked John.

"They're ghosts. Special ghosts without any feet. Tutu says they were warriors or priests or *ali'i*. An *ali'i* is a chief."

"Ah," said John.

"Anyway, sometimes these special ghosts come back to the land of the living. They come at night, marching in a line. Sometimes they come silently. Sometimes they march to the sound of a drum or a nose flute—scary, yeah? People think they're dangerous."

"Did Tutu ever actually see the Night Marchers?"

"She says she never did. But she heard their music," said Kalani.

John brushed the light brown hair out of his eyes. "When I was a cabin boy on a ship, I saw some strange things. I'd just as soon not see any Night Marchers."

Kalani shuddered. "Me neither."

The boys bent down to pick up the slop bucket again and walked slowly.

"Careful, now," said Kalani as they stopped at a wooden fence. "Lift it up. One, two, three…" They slipped the bucket handle onto a hook out of reach of the dog and small children.

"Whew," said John. "Stinky stuff, that garbage."

"You'll get used to it," said Kalani. "Better not leave it in the house, stink the house up too, yeah? The pig man will pick it up tomorrow. He'll come before we catch the horse trolley for school."

"Boys!" a man's voice called. "Homework time!"

"Come on," said John. "I think that's Mr. Wilson calling us. I still have to do my sums."

"And I have to do a dumb old report," said Kalani. "About Kamehameha. I get sick of all that history. But Teacher says now that we don't have a king or a queen ruling over us, we need to study so we don't forget who we are. She's half Hawaiian, you know."

"Come, lads," called Mr. Wilson. "Hurry up."

Kalani slapped his hand against the fence, his face dark with anger. "Always nagging us. Always chores or studying or something. It's no fun living with Teacher. I always have to do my homework. Some day, believe me, some day I'm going to run away," Kalani sulked.

Then he brightened up. "We still have to feed Spotty. Come on, John. You can help."

Kalani led John into the kitchen. He picked up the bowl of table scraps Mrs. Wilson had saved for the dog and set it outside the door. "Here,

12

Spotty," he called.

A small, mixed-breed *poi* dog with short brown and white hair came bounding around the corner of the house. He jumped up on Kalani, wagging his tail, before diving into the food.

"That's surely a cute dog," said John.

"He's been my best friend these past two years," said Kalani. "Ever since I moved here." He bent down and ruffled Spotty's ears.

Then he put his head down near the dog. "We'll play tomorrow, Spotty. I've got homework to do now."

Spotty didn't pay any attention to Kalani. He just kept his nose in the bowl, gulping the food.

2. Homework Time

Kalani led John to the kitchen sink. He pushed the handle of the pump up and down while John squished strong, yellow lye soap through his fingers and rinsed it off. Then John pumped water for Kalani. They dried their hands on a not-too-dirty towel hanging from a nail.

John put his fingers under his nose.

"Still stinks," he muttered.

"Never mind," said Kalani. "Come into the dining room. If we're late, the Wilsons will get mad."

Six children—Japanese, Chinese, Portuguese, and Caucasian—were already bent over their books around the long dining room table. Two had pencils and paper, working on sums or English grammar. Two were sounding out words in a McGuffey reader, their fingers moving along the lines of print.

Tutu, who played grandmother to everybody, sat at one end of the table helping two younger children learn their ABCs.

Kalani searched a shelf and found his Hawaiian storybook and John's arithmetic book. On his way back to the table, a skinny white girl tripped him, causing him to stumble and almost drop the books. Quickly, so Tutu would not see, he thumped the back of her head with his finger. She glared at him and stuck out her tongue as he sat down beside John.

"Where's Mrs. Wilson?" John whispered.

"She's getting the small kids ready for bed," said Kalani. "Teacher is helping her. You might as well get used to it. With all those *keiki* around, you're not going to see Mama—or Teacher— very much."

"Teacher is Mrs. Wilson's daughter?" asked John.

"That is right. Mrs. Wilson and Miss Wilson. But we call them 'Mama' and 'Teacher.'"

"How many children live here?" whispered John, spreading his copybook open beside his arithmetic book.

"Eight of us in school, and seven small ones that stay home. We only had six small *keiki* until last month. Then we got this teensy baby. She cries all the time. She makes my head ache. I don't know what's wrong with her."

"Where did she come from?" asked John.

"I don't know." Kalani made a face. "Mr. and

Mrs. Wilson—they take in just anybody."

"It's a good thing they do," smiled John. "If they hadn't taken me in, I wouldn't have any place to go. I wonder why they do that."

"Mr. Wilson says back in England his folks were in prison because they couldn't pay their bills. Somebody else raised him, and he promised God that he would take care of *keiki* when he grew up."

"It must cost a lot of money to feed all these kids."

"Yes, I guess it does. But Mr. Wilson has a good job downtown. And Mama, she's Hawaiian you know, she owns land. So I guess they have enough money."

"Did Teacher find the other children the same way she found me?" asked John. "Did they just show up at school the way I did?"

"Some of them did. And some of them, their relatives couldn't take care of them so they brought them to the Wilsons. They came different ways."

"Quiet, boys," said Tutu, putting her finger to her lips. "Study time."

Kalani made a face. John bent over his arithmetic book, trying to see the figures. Kalani turned up the wick in the kerosene lamp nearest him to a just-right glow.

Down the hall, the tiny baby still fussed. Over in a corner, a cricket chirped.

"I can't think with all that noise: that baby squalling and the cricket squeaking," grumbled

Kalani. He slammed his book shut and pushed his chair back.

Tutu looked up from the ABC chart. "Never mind," she said. "The baby cannot help, you know. And the cricket? Well, a cricket in the house is good luck. We're going to be blessed."

Kalani glared at Tutu. She smiled back at him. He pulled his chair back to the table and opened his book again. He could feel his angry thoughts going away; Tutu had that special way about her. She always made him feel good.

Kalani leaned his shiny brown face close to John's pale, freckled one. "Let's get this homework over with," he grinned. "If we work hard, maybe Tutu will tell us a story, yeah?"

Kalani wrote "Kamehameha" at the top of his copybook. Under it, he wrote his own name and the date, December 10, 1896.

For the moment, he forgot about Night Marchers. If he had known the future, he would have been worried.

3. The Magical Breadfruit Tree

"Line up," said Kalani in a bossy voice. "Lottie Jane, Chu Lee, John, Toshi, Morio, Leilani, Kimo. All of you, line up. Let me check on you."

All the school-age children obeyed him, lining up in the kitchen near the sink. Kalani walked down the line, doing his job as oldest boy in the family. He checked each child's teeth. "You didn't brush, Lottie Jane," he told the pouting girl who had tripped him at the table.

"Did too," she said, sticking out her tongue.

"It doesn't look like it," said Kalani. "For an eleven-year-old *haole* girl, a white girl, you sure don't know much. Do it again."

Lottie Jane stuck up her nose and flounced off to the sink.

Kalani checked everyone's hands and fingernails, even John's.

"Sorry I have to treat you like a baby, John," Kalani said. "But those are the rules."

"Lots of rules in this house," said John.

"Yes. Too many rules. I get sick of it," agreed Kalani. "It wasn't like that in my real family."

The baby fussed from the far end of the hall.

"That baby," said Kalani. "I wish she would shut up."

A voice called to them from a nearby room. "Ready?"

"Ready!" shouted the children, scrambling into the room where Tutu waited. The eight school-age children pulled up pillows around her feet. Shushing and poking, they quieted each other down.

"Let's see," Tutu said softly. "What shall it be tonight?"

"Night Marchers," said Kalani immediately.

"No. That's a daytime story," said Tutu, shaking her head. "We don't want to talk about them at night. They might hear us and come through the house."

Kalani nodded. He didn't want Night Marchers coming through the house, either.

Tutu gazed out the window into the darkness. "You know that breadfruit tree in the yard? There used to be another one by Nuʻuanu Stream, down near Chinatown. A long time ago something strange happened to that tree."

Tutu's round, brown face shone in the dim lamplight as she began the story. The children snuggled against each other, ready to listen.

"Once, long, long ago, Wākea and his wife, Papa, lived far back in Kalihi Valley. They were so happy living there because they had everything they needed: vines and flowers to wear as clothes, and all sorts of tasty food growing in the fields and swimming in the ocean.

"One day, while Papa..."

"Papa is a woman?" asked John.

"Yes. Papa is the name of a Hawaiian god-woman."

"Shhhhh!" said all the children.

"John doesn't know about Hawaiian gods," said Tutu to the children. "He's just come here. Be patient. Now, one day Papa heard shouting and saw that men had tied up Wākea and were leading him along a path. Papa knew what they were going to do. She knew that they were building a fire in the oven down in the *heiau*.

"Let him go," she screamed.

"Never," said the men. 'We caught him stealing food out of the chief's garden.'

Well, Papa saw a huge, absolutely enormous breadfruit tree growing right by the stream. She had an idea. She began kissing Wākea and whirling him around and around, and then... the tree opened. And Papa and Wākea jumped inside.

"Papa magically opened the tree on the other side. Hand in hand, Papa and Wākea ran up the mountainside, up, up, up Kalihi Valley."

"And then the men chopped down the tree,"

said Lottie Jane.

Kalani pushed Lottie Jane. "Know it all," he hissed.

Lottie Jane pushed him back. "Bully!" she said, pinching him.

"Quiet, children," continued Tutu, patting Kalani on the shoulder and frowning at Lottie Jane. "Yes. And they carved that tree into a statue of a goddess. People who worshipped the statue were filled with power. They could win land from other people."

Kalani's eyes widened. "I read about that for my report tonight. Kamehameha took the statue from O'ahu to Maui. Maybe that's why he was able to beat all the other chiefs."

"Perhaps so," said Tutu, nodding her head slowly. "Anyway, Wākea and Papa were safe from the men. By the time the men cut down that tree, Wākea and Papa were far, far up Kalihi Valley."

She smiled at the children. "Good story?" she asked.

"Good story!" they all agreed, clapping their hands before picking up their pillows.

"Now, off to bed," said Tutu. "School tomorrow."

4. The Oldest Boy

Lottie Jane obediently went to her room, undressed, and slipped on her nightgown. She climbed into bed, but she had a hard time getting to sleep. An awful smell kept her awake. No matter which way she turned, she couldn't get away from it. She never did find the rag Kalani put inside her pillowcase. A rag dipped in hog slop.

Kalani, John, and Chu Lee were in another bedroom down the hall. Kalani and John had their heads at one end of the bed, and Chu Lee had his head at the other. The legs of the three boys tangled around each other in the middle.

Kalani smiled in the dark, thinking about Lottie Jane and the stinky rag. *Serves her right*, he chuckled to himself.

He turned to John. "Do you think a wooden statue really has special powers?"

"I don't know," said John after a moment. "Maybe."

Kalani wiggled around, trying to find more room in the bed. "Do you ever miss your family?"

"Sure, I miss them something terrible," said John. "But they're back in Boston. I try not to think about them."

"Why did you leave home?"

"Times were hard. There wasn't enough food for everybody, and I was the oldest. So I hired on as the cabin boy on a sailing ship."

"You were the oldest. So you know how it feels," said Kalani.

"What do you mean?"

"I'm thirteen."

"Me, too. Well, almost," said John truthfully.

"Well, since I'm the oldest in this house," said Kalani, "anytime there's anything really hard to do, or, or... anything, it's got to be me that does it. I'm sick of it."

"Yeah. But at least you've got a home."

"Some home. Before the cholera got my folks and my brothers, I had a real home. My folks cared about me. My brothers, too. But the Wilsons don't care about me. If I ran away, these people wouldn't even miss me. At least not until chore time."

The baby was still fussing down the hall.

"Particularly now with that bawling baby around. Mama—she doesn't even talk to me now, except when she wants me to do something. I hate that baby."

John patted Kalani's shoulder. "Maybe things will get better," he said.

Kalani didn't answer. Two years ago he was the youngest of three boys. If there was one piece of candy, his father made his brothers give it to him. If he skinned his knee, his mother always made it better. She'd lick her fingers and put the spit on the skinned place. Then she'd give him a hug. Here at the Wilsons, no one cared if he skinned his knee. And practically no one got hugs.

John and Chu Lee were breathing deeply. Kalani knew they were asleep.

In the daytime, in front of other people, Kalani had to act tough: bossy and sure of himself. But now, in the dark, he let himself cry. The sobs shook his shoulders. What should he do? Should he run away? All he did was work and take care of the little kids. He was sure the Wilsons didn't love him. But if he ran away, where would he go?

5. Plans for Nuʻuanu Valley

The next day, Kalani and John sat under a huge banyan tree in the schoolyard, eating their lunches. Chu Lee and another Chinese boy, Eddie, who lived in Chinatown, sat under the tree with them. Even though Kalani and John were thirteen and Chu Lee and Eddie were only ten, they were all friends.

Chu Lee and Eddie ate rice and vegetables packed in a metal lunch box. They ate with chopsticks; Kalani and John picked up their sandwiches with their hands.

Eddie said, "Uncle Han is taking the grocery wagon up Nuʻuanu Valley next Saturday to get bamboo for kites. He says we can go too."

"Wow!" said Kalani. "That would be great." Then he looked glum. "But old Mr. Wilson probably will say we can't go. Saturday's the day for special chores. There's always a lot to do."

He slammed the lid of his lunch box, angry at the thought of Saturday chores.

Two girls from Chinatown sat under the tree near the boys. Ruth was Chinese. Yumi was Japanese. Ruth had a scar on her face from falling into a cooking fire, but she had learned to use actor's face paint to hide the scar almost completely.

Kalani looked at her over his sandwich. She really was a pretty girl with that scar covered up.

"What are you boys planning to do?" asked Ruth, moving closer.

"Oh, Ruth. You have to get in on everything," said Eddie. Ruth and Eddie Wong were twins. They both wore braids and dressed alike in long, loose blue pants and cotton jackets. They lived above Wong's grocery store. Yumi, the Japanese girl, lived above her mother's noodle shop a couple of blocks from Ruth. Her father was a fisherman.

"Well, why shouldn't we get in on everything?" Ruth asked. "Right, Yumi?" She and the Japanese girl giggled. They put their chopsticks into their lunch boxes and closed the lids.

"This is boys only," said Eddie. "Uncle Han said so."

"We'll just see about that," said Ruth. She and Yumi stood up. Ruth brushed off her Chinese pants and Yumi straightened her plantation dress.

"I guess you can ask Uncle Han," said Eddie.

Kalani jumped up angrily. "Why do you give in to her, Eddie?" he shouted. "If you want it to be boys only, then make it boys only!" He grabbed his lunch box and stormed into the school. When he glanced back, he saw that Ruth and Yumi were giggling.

"Let them giggle," muttered Kalani. "Silly girls." But really, he did want Ruth to come along on the trip. He thought Ruth was nice. He was just acting angry to get attention.

6. Sneaking Out

When Sunday came, Kalani lay in bed with his eyes closed. He didn't want to go to church. His throat was a teensy bit scratchy, so he decided he would play sick.

He swallowed. His throat was not really sore, but scratchy enough that he thought he could fool the Wilsons.

He opened his eyes a tiny slit and looked around. John and Chu Lee were already up, putting on their Sunday clothes. Mama came into the room, her tall, broad body almost filling the doorway. Chu Lee and John wiggled past her to go to breakfast.

"What's the matter, Kalani? It's time to get ready for church."

"I don't feel good," Kalani moaned, keeping his voice low and pitiful.

Mama laid her broad hand on his forehead. "Hmmm. You don't feel hot. Open your mouth and say ahhh."

Kalani did.

"Your throat's a bit pinker than usual. But I think you can make it through church, yeah?"

Kalani swung his legs over the edge of the bed.

Mama added, "Of course, after church, since you're not feeling well, you'll have to spend the rest of the day in bed."

Curses, thought Kalani.

He pulled on his knee pants, buttoned his starchy-stiff Sunday shirt, and went downstairs to breakfast.

All the family was there, dressed in their best clothes. All six little children. All eight big children. An older child sat between each little one. The big children tied the younger one's bibs and helped them with their spoons.

Teacher laughed and joked with the children while she stirred her coffee. Mr. Wilson, tall and thin, sat next to Mama, tall and fat. Lottie Jane bounced and patted the fussy baby while everyone else ate eggs and toast and jam.

"I really should stay home," Kalani said, thinking of the long church service. He coughed a little, then sneezed.

"Have to do better than that, my boy," Mr. Wilson chuckled. Using his long slender fingers, he swished his toast around his plate, scooping up the

rest of his egg.

"Delicious breakfast, my dear," he said, smiling at his wife.

He rose and turned to Kalani. "Church will do you more good than laying about," he said, patting him on the head.

"Come along now, everybody," Teacher said. "Clean hands, clean faces. See to them, won't you Kalani? I'll help the small ones with their hair bows and such."

"Yes, Teacher," said Kalani. *Chores*, he thought, *then church, then bed*. What a miserable day this would be!

That afternoon Kalani lay on his bed. His sore throat was gone. His fake cough and sneeze were gone. He felt fine.

I wish Ruth and Eddie went to our church, he thought, counting the cracks in the ceiling. *We could have fun together. But they go to that church where they speak Chinese.*

Outside, chickens scratched and clucked. Kalani turned over and looked through the window at the breadfruit tree blowing in the breeze. The sky was deep blue behind white fluffy clouds. It was too nice to stay inside.

I could sneak out, he thought.

He got up, leaned out the second-story window, and looked down. The ground seemed awfully far away.

The breadfruit tree was just out of reach.

Maybe if I lean way out... he thought.

He climbed up on the windowsill. By leaning out and giving a little jump, he was able to reach a branch. But the branch was too thin to hold him.

Kalani hit every branch on his way to the ground. He lay there a moment, shaking his head, dizzy. Spotty came bounding around the side of the house. He licked Kalani's face, whimpering and wagging his tail.

Kalani rolled away from the dog, putting his hands up to his face. Then he sat up and looked around. No one came out of the house. Maybe Spotty was the only one who had heard him fall.

He poked all along his right arm with one finger. He poked all along his left arm with another finger. Then he checked his legs. No bones were broken.

"Come on, Spotty," he whispered. "Let's go fishing."

7. The Shark

Kalani tore down the dirt street with Spotty chasing after him. He dodged a horse and buggy carrying a man and woman dressed in their Sunday best. Then three women on horseback raced past, their long colorful dresses flowing behind them. No one paid any attention as Kalani sped along, hoping no one saw him. He didn't want anyone to tell the Wilsons where he was. He wanted to go fishing!

He ran a long time before stopping to catch his breath. He gave Spotty a loving pat as he looked back. The house was out of sight. No one was chasing him.

Another twenty minutes of fast walking led him to a fishing pier on the ocean.

Spotty, delighted, immediately snuffled up a sand crab. Then he romped with another dog,

CROCI

putting his head down, barking, jumping, and twisting around.

"You're glad to get out of that fenced yard, huh, Spotty?" Kalani laughed. "I know how you feel."

Then Kalani remembered that he hadn't brought his fishing tackle.

Just as well, he thought. *If I'd stopped to get it, somebody would have seen me. But what can I use?*

He searched along a ditch at the side of the road and found a stick. A little further along there was a bit of string. But he needed a hook. What could he use for a hook?

An old fisherman was sitting on the pier watching Kalani. "Need a hook, boy?" he asked.

"Yes, sir," said Kalani.

"Here, take one of mine," the fisherman said, reaching into his basket. "I've plenty." The fisherman was a wiry Hawaiian. His shoulder-length, curly black hair was streaked with gray.

He motioned for Kalani to sit down beside him. "You need bait, too," he said, handing him a small piece of fish.

While Kalani stuck the chum on the hook, the old man talked. "I used to throw net," he explained. "But now, my joints getting creaky, you know. Nice to stay dry on the shore. I don't throw net like I did when I was young."

Kalani grinned. Then his line jiggled.

"Think you got something, boy," said the old

man. "Pull it in. Let's see."

But when Kalani pulled in the line, there was no fish. Only an empty hook.

"Danged crabs," said the old man. "Steal bait all the time. Well, try again, boy." His frizzy hair fell over his face as he pulled another bit of chum from his basket.

They sat together in comfortable silence, their lines dangling off the pier side by side. The waves lapped against the shore: swish, swish, swish. Mynah birds jabbered to each other in the palm trees.

Spotty lay down beside Kalani, panting from his dog games, and laid his chin upon his paws.

"You Hawaiian, boy?" the man asked.

"Yes. I am."

"Good to be Hawaiian. Not like the old days, though. Too much change."

"How do you mean?"

"All these buildings. Streets. Even a trolley. Used to be, only grass houses. Small, those houses, but big enough, yeah?"

"I wish I lived back in the old days," said Kalani. "No school. No homework."

The old Hawaiian man smiled. "Those days long gone, boy. Not see them again, I think."

Suddenly Kalani felt a tug on his string. "A strike!" he said.

"Pull easy, boy, set the hook," the man said, placing his hand over Kalani's. "Not too quick, steady, steady..."

Together they battled the fish. Kalani could feel the fish through the string, struggling, diving deep, then leaping out of the water. A moment later a hammerhead shark lay flapping on the pier.

"Hey, that's a beauty, boy. Long as your arm, almost. Good eating. Your family be proud of you, yeah?"

8. A Present for Ruth

The old man took some newspaper from his basket and began to wrap the big fish.

Kalani knew he couldn't take the fish home to the Wilsons. If he did, they would know he had sneaked out of his room to go fishing.

"Do you want it?" he asked the old man.

The man shook his head. "Nah, boy. I've caught my fill for the day. You take it on home. Make your daddy proud."

"Well... all right," said Kalani. "And thanks... for everything."

"Glad to help," the man said, turning back to face the ocean.

"Come on, Spotty," said Kalani. "Let's go."

Slowly, they walked along the dirt road. "What shall we do?" Kalani wondered. "Who would want a nice hammerhead?"

Spotty jumped in a circle and barked.

Kalani wandered on a little ways before he realized where his feet were taking him. Wong's Grocery.

"Maybe Ruth would like the fish," he said to Spotty.

Spotty barked and chased his tail.

"Silly dog! Stop it!" laughed Kalani. "This is serious. I don't want her to see me. I'll just write a note on the wrapper and leave it inside the store."

Kalani dug down in his pants pocket and pulled out a pretty silvery shell, a yellow marble that you could look through and see the sky turn green, a lucky penny, and finally, the stub of a pencil. He sucked on the pencil lead a second, then began to write:

"To Ruth from Your Friend, Kalani."

Then he changed his mind. *If she doesn't like fish she'll think I'm teasing her. I better scratch out my name real good.*

He scribbled over his name until he made a hole in the paper. Then he re-wrapped the still-wiggling fish and trotted off to Wong's Grocery.

No one was near the front of the store, but he could hear voices in the rear. He gingerly placed the wrapped fish on the counter. Then he and Spotty ran across the street, hiding in a dark doorway to watch and wait.

A huge black cat marched through the store holding its tail high like a flag. It jumped up on the counter and sniffed at a candy jar. At the other end of the counter, the newspaper began to wiggle. The cat sniffed the package, then rubbed the top of its head against the newspaper.

Sticking its nose under one corner of the paper, the cat pushed away the wrapper. Before Kalani realized what was happening, the cat sank its teeth into the fish and jumped down, dragging the fish to the floor. Holding its head high, the cat struggled to carry the fish, its tail dragging on one side, its head on the other. Stiffening its neck, the cat trotted proudly down the street.

Kalani tried to hold Spotty back, but the excited dog broke loose from his grip. Barking, he tore out of the hiding place and chased the cat— and the fish—all the way to the harbor.

Kalani noticed Eddie and Ruth come running down the street from the other direction. He stayed hidden in the doorway.

"I beat you," said Eddie.

"You did not," said Ruth.

"Did!" said Eddie, as they ran into the store.

"What's this?" asked Ruth, picking up the newspaper. "Look, it's got my name written on it."

She lifted the wet newspaper to her nose. "*Eeeeuw!*" she exclaimed.

Eddie looked at the writing. "It says, 'To Ruth from Your Friend,' but the name's been rubbed out."

"Some friend, yeah?" laughed Ruth.

"Maybe it used to have a fish in it," said Eddie.

Ruth wadded it up. "Yeah, maybe so. Well, I'll take it out back for the cooking fire. That's all it's good for."

9. Caught!

Kalani felt foolish. Maybe Ruth would have liked a hammerhead shark, but nobody would like a piece of smelly newspaper! He was glad he had rubbed out his name. He sank back into the shadows, his face burning hot. He must not, absolutely must not let Ruth see him there.

He held perfectly still until he was sure Eddie and Ruth weren't coming back to the front of the store. Then he ran up the dirt street in the other direction, away from Spotty and the huge black cat and the fish.

When he reached home Mr. Wilson was standing on the *lānai*, his hands behind his back. He teetered up and down on his toes, his face red with anger.

"Where have you been?" he barked at Kalani.

"I... I..."

"You were told to stay in your room," said

Mr. Wilson, grabbing Kalani by the sleeve. "Now, you can just take out the slop bucket by yourself, young man. And no supper for you tonight."

Mr. Wilson stormed back into the house and slammed the door.

Kalani struggled to pick up the heavy slop bucket. Spotty came from around the side of the house and licked his hand, whimpering.

"I've had enough," said Kalani, letting loose of the bucket handle. "Spotty, let's get out of here."

Kalani and Spotty raced up the street, away from the ocean, toward the mountains.

Soon they were climbing through woods thick with bushes and vines. Kalani faced a steep bank, looking for a way up. He grabbed an exposed root and dug his toes into the dirt. He clutched clumps of grass and rocks to pull himself along.

Spotty scrambled and slipped, slid down, and scrambled again, his tongue hanging out as he panted after Kalani.

The sun was almost down, and Kalani had never been out by himself at night before. Spirits came out at night, and it wasn't safe.

"Where can we spend the night, Spotty?"

"Ruff," barked Spotty.

"Maybe we can find a cave."

They slid down a steep slope and started up the other side of the ravine. Then Kalani's foot got caught under a rock.

"Ow!" he said, grabbing his ankle. "I'm

caught, Spotty. And my ankle—it feels like I've twisted it."

Spotty sniffed around Kalani's foot, trying to help.

Kalani pulled and wiggled, but he couldn't get his foot loose. "Stay close to me, Spotty," he said, pulling the dog to his side. "It's getting dark."

The boy and the dog huddled together. The wind blew through the trees, making a scary, rustling sound. Something waved back and forth. Was it a tree branch... or was it a ghost?

Kalani hugged Spotty against his chest, trying to look in all directions at once to see if anything was out there in the dark to hurt him. He glanced again and again at the dark thing waving back and forth.

His foot throbbed for a while. Then it lost feeling as the blood supply was cut off. Kalani smoothed out the grass around him, trying to find a comfortable place to lie down. He looked again at the dark thing waving back and forth. It still had not moved away, but it had not moved any closer. Kalani decided it must be a tree branch. He relaxed.

Then Spotty started to bark.

Kalani tapped him on the nose. "Hush, Spotty. You're not helping any."

But Spotty heard something and he wouldn't stop barking.

Something was coming through the bushes. Kalani could see a dark form stumbling down the ravine toward him. His hair stood up. His throat got tight. Then he heard a familiar voice.

"Kalani! I thought I'd never find you."

"John!"

John bent down and hugged Kalani. "Good thing Spotty was barking. I might not have found you if he hadn't made so much noise. Come on," he said. "The Wilsons are worried about you."

"They are?" Kalani was surprised.

"Of course they are. When they found your room empty, they looked all over the neighborhood for you. Then when it started getting dark, they had to get the little kids to bed. I said I'd check up here for you."

"Weren't you afraid to go out in the dark?"

"Nah. I did it all the time when I was on the ship. Now, come on. Let's get back to the house."

"My foot's caught. I can't move."

John knelt down. He tugged on the rock that held Kalani's foot. It wouldn't budge.

John dug out the dirt around the rock to try to get it loose. As John shoved the rock a little to one side, the feeling started coming back into Kalani's foot and ankle. It hurt really bad.

Kalani helped John, working with both hands to dig out the dirt and push the rock. He was working so hard he didn't hear the steady beat of a drum coming up the mountain. And of course, he didn't hear any footsteps: the marchers had no feet.

Night Marchers!

10. Through The Lava Tube

Kalani clung to John as they watched a row of torches come toward them.

"Get down!" said Kalani. "Don't let them see you."

John lay flat in the grass beside Kalani.

The row of Night Marchers, eight or ten men dressed in loincloth *malos*, came steadily up the mountain. They did not look to the right or to the left. They marched to the slow beat of the drum. Boom. Boom. Boom.

When the Marchers were almost upon them, Spotty began to bark. Still the Marchers did not look at them. But when the first one got to Kalani, he reached down and shoved aside the rock holding Kalani's foot as easily as if it were a leaf. Then he grabbed Kalani around the waist and lifted him up.

Kalani stiffened. Was the Marcher going to kill him?

Behind him he heard John call out, "Jesus. Jesus, help us."

The Marcher never turned around. He never missed a step. He carried Kalani down the ravine, up the slope on the other side, and into a cave.

The flickering torchlight cast odd shadows on the bumpy walls of the tunnel. Kalani knew this was a lava tube. He knew the bumps in the walls weren't really wild animals or spirits or hurtful things. But they surely looked like they were.

At first he was so scared he couldn't breathe. But little by little, he relaxed. He could hardly feel the Marcher's arms holding him, but he didn't feel like he was going to fall. He felt oddly comfortable. Even his twisted ankle, so painful moments before, had completely stopped hurting.

He wondered what had happened to John. He hoped he was all right. As for Spotty, he could hear him back at the entrance to the lava tube, still barking.

The barking grew fainter and fainter. The Night Marchers pushed on and on, through the torch-lit, shadowy tunnel. Would they never stop?

Kalani remembered something Teacher had told him. Long ago, Hawaiians had a special use for caves. They wrapped the bones of dead kings and chiefs in *tapa* cloth and they buried them in the lava tubes. Kalani shuddered. Would he see bones in the flickering light of the torches? Worse, would the Night Marchers wrap HIM in *tapa* cloth and leave him there?

The Marcher's body swayed back and forth. Kalani fought to stay awake.

Suddenly, the Marchers stopped.

Thud! He landed on packed dirt. Was he still in the lava tube? He seemed to be in some sort of room.

He could hear people moving around. By pale light he could see two huge men exit through a rounded doorway. Then all was silent.

Slowly, he became aware of someone in the room with him. He could hear breathing. For a long time he sat very still, not daring to move. At last, he grew braver.

"Who's there?" he whispered.

A whisper came back to him through the dark.

"It's me. John. Is that you, Kalani?"

"Oh, John. I'm so glad you're here!"

Kalani crawled toward the voice. The boys hugged each other.

Kalani said, "I was afraid they would kill you! Tutu says the only way a person escapes Night Marchers is if one of them is his relative."

"So the one that carried you off was your ancestor?"

"I guess so. But the one who brought you couldn't have been your relative."

"Not hardly. I just got to Hawai'i a few weeks

ago. Hmmm…"

"What do you suppose saved you?" Kalani wondered out loud.

"I think… I think I know," said John. "I prayed. The preacher always says if we have troubles, to pray and Jesus will help us."

"Maybe I should have paid more attention in church," said Kalani. "It's a good thing you listened!" They fell silent again. Kalani could hear several people moving around outside.

"Where are we?" asked John.

Kalani said, "It's so dark I'm not sure. But the floor of this place is packed earth." Kalani crawled to the edge of the floor and patted the walls. "I can feel grass walls and the sticks that hold them up. This is an old-style Hawaiian house, I think."

John crawled over to the doorway and looked out.

"It's dark outside. Nighttime. Some men are over by a fire. Oops—somebody's coming." John backed away from the door.

A man with a torch brought a wooden platter of food. Without a word, he handed it to John, then left.

"Did you see his feet?" asked Kalani.

"Yes. He had feet… so he's not a Night Marcher. But he was dressed in a loincloth, just like the Night Marchers."

"Maybe they're pretending like it's the olden

days," said Kalani. "Or maybe they're actors in a play or something."

"Maybe so," said John. "But I know one thing, this isn't pretend food. And I'm hungry."

"Me too," agreed Kalani.

He began scooping up *poi* with his fingers, and John copied him. They nibbled at the fish. It tasted good.

Kalani got up and looked out the door. What he saw worried him.

John smacked his lips. "Is this great food, or am I just hungry?"

"Both, I think. But I don't like the looks of this."

"What do you mean? Those men are being good to us, feeding us and all."

"Yes. But did you notice the man outside the door? It's like he's guarding us. I don't think these men are in a play. I think this is real. And I think we're prisoners."

11. Where Are We? When Is It?

Early the next morning, men began to stick their heads inside the hut. One after another they stared at Kalani and John, chattering in Hawaiian, pointing their fingers, laughing, and shaking their heads.

"They say we're funny looking." Kalani translated for John.

"Well, I'm happy they have something to laugh at," grumbled John. "Why don't they just go away and leave us alone?"

"They say we're the first people they have seen with clothes like this," said Kalani. "I wonder where they have been."

Kalani and John stood up and walked over to the door. The men moved away, then sat down in a half circle a little way from the hut. They watched the doorway.

"Look," said John, pointing outside at the sun-filled village. "The whole place is just like this house. All made of grass. And there aren't any roads or horses or carts. It seems just like..."

"Just like a Hawaiian village a long time ago," said Kalani. "Teacher told me what Hawai'i was like before the foreigners came. She has a book with paintings in it. Some sailors painted them when they came to Hawai'i a hundred years ago."

Kalani looked at John and shook his head. "John, I don't know how this happened, but it's like... like we went back in time. Like that lava tube has one end in 1896 and the other end way back a long time ago."

"I don't see how that's possible," said John. "I still think this is just a stage set or a show or... or something."

"That doesn't seem likely, either," said Kalani. "But I sure don't understand what is going on."

Slowly, a man walked over to the men sitting on the ground. He was carrying a little stack of mats. He set them down and talked with the other men for a long time. At last, he picked up the mats and walked toward the door.

He came inside, out of the bright sunshine into the dimly lit room. When his eyes got used to the dimness, he looked the boys up and down. Then he walked all around them, touching John's woven cloth shirt, poking at the buckle of Kalani's belt.

"See, my belt works like this," said Kalani, unbuckling the belt and buckling it again.

The man dropped the mats. He showed them how to spread two mats on the floor and use two more for covers.

Then he pointed to the belt and pointed to himself.

"You want to try it on?" asked Kalani. He laughed as he tried to fasten the belt around the big Hawaiian's waist above his *malo*. The man's waist was twice as big as Kalani's. The man took the belt and wrapped it around his leg. He buckled it, then smiled, his white teeth gleaming in the dim room.

Then he motioned for the boys to follow him out of the hut, over to the circle of men.

All the men were interested in how the buckle worked. They gathered around to try out the strange piece of clothing.

Then the man motioned to the boys to follow him.

Not far from the hut, children were playing. Boys slid stones along the ground, trying to scoot them between two stakes. Girls dipped hollow leaf stems into soapy water and blew bubbles into the air. Little children chased each other in a game of tag.

"Wonderful!" said Kalani, beginning to relax. "Everybody's playing. Nobody's working. This is great!"

A crowd gathered. Everyone was talking and

laughing and pointing at John. They made a circle around the boys.

Kalani said, "They're surprised at the way you look. They say they've never seen a boy with freckled white skin and light brown hair."

Some of the older boys poked at John. Then they began to push him around.

The man with the belted leg stepped over and stood beside John. He yelled at the boys and they backed away. Then he spoke to Kalani.

"He says he doesn't know where we came from, but we better not try to hurt anyone. He says he will tell the boys not to hurt us, either. He says if we're going to stay here, we ought to try to be part of the village and play the games," Kalani interpreted for John.

"What does he mean, if we're going to stay here?" questioned John. "Maybe I don't want to stay here."

"I am not sure we have a choice," said Kalani. "Look around you, John."

12. The Sliding Hill

Many of the women wore *tapa* cloths for skirts. Men wore *malos*. Very young children wore nothing at all. Only Kalani and John wore button-front shirts and knee pants.

The houses were all made of *pili* grass. Each one seemed to have only one room. Footpaths led through the village. There were no roads.

"I think we're stuck," said Kalani. "I'm sure this village is in the past; I'm not sure what year. The Night Marchers brought us here, but I really don't know how we will get back to our own time."

"That's hard to believe," said John. "Maybe these people are just in a valley somewhere. Maybe they are way back somewhere, and they've never seen people from Honolulu or people from other countries."

"Maybe," said Kalani, raising his eyebrows.

"But I don't think so."

At the far end of the village, a stone wall about as tall as the boys enclosed a square piece of land.

"What do you suppose those walls are for?" John asked softly.

Kalani murmured in response. "It's too far away to see very well. Let's try to find out later."

John looked around him, puzzled. "Do you notice there aren't any horses? Just pigs and chickens. It's very strange. Not real."

"It is real," said Kalani, nodding his head. "When the Hawaiians first came to these islands on their double-hulled canoes, they brought pigs and chickens. They didn't have horses back then. Horses came on the big foreign ships later. This place is exactly like I read about in my Hawaiian storybooks. Exactly like it was on O'ahu before Kamehameha."

"Back in the 1700s?"

"Yes. More than a hundred years ago," said Kalani.

"You mean...?"

"I don't know how they did it, but somehow those Night Marchers took us a long way through that lava tube. I think they took us right back to the last century."

"Maybe you're right," said John. His white face got even whiter; his freckles stood out like flecks of mud on a starched Sunday shirt. A hundred years ago? That was scary.

Kalani felt a hand on his shoulder. The man

wearing the belt around his leg pushed the two boys down the path. Other boys were laughing and shouting.

"What now?" asked John. "I wish I could speak Hawaiian. It's hard not knowing what they're saying."

"They're talking about a sliding hill."

"Really? I wonder what that is," said John. "Well, I guess we'll find out soon enough."

They came to the bottom of a hill. Boys were sliding down the grassy slope on ti leaves.

"That looks fun," said John. "Let's try it."

The first couple of times down the hill, Kalani and John fell off the leaves. It really was harder than it looked. But soon they were able to go from top to bottom as well as any of the other boys. They whooped and swooped and flew down the hill.

When the group of boys tired of sliding, they walked back to the village. Some lay down to rest. Some spun wooden tops. Others arm-wrestled.

Kalani flopped down on the ground in a shady spot, his white shirt covered with dirt, the seat of his pants muddy. He was glad Tutu couldn't see him.

"This is great," said John, stretching out on the ground beside Kalani. "No school. No homework. No chores. Just playtime all day."

"It seems too good to be true," said Kalani.

"Yes, I know. But we might as well enjoy it," said John. "You were complaining about chores.

Now you don't have to do any at all."

John turned over on his back and put his hands behind his head. "I don't know how we got to this place. I don't know how we got to this century, either. But the games are fun, and the people feed us. They're even getting used to my white skin. I think this is going to be a good life for us."

"I hope so," said Kalani, but he felt uneasy.

He wished he had paid more attention to his Hawaiian storybooks. He had studied about daily life in ancient Hawai'i. He had even read about these games. He remembered that some things in old Hawai'i seemed wonderful. He also remembered that some things seemed terrible.

He wished he could remember more about it. Just what was it that had seemed so bad?

Before they went to bed that night, a different man brought them two *malos*. He asked Kalani a lot of questions and listened carefully to his answers.

After he left, Kalani explained. "He says it's time we dressed like them. He asked me where we came from. He asked why we wore such strange clothes. I told him we came from far away. I didn't know what else to tell him."

John nodded. "It's pretty hard to explain something when we don't understand it ourselves."

Kalani took off his dirty shirt and pants, rolled them up, and quickly wound one of the *malos* around his body.

John unbuttoned his shirt and picked up the other *malo*. "How do you put these things on?" he asked.

Kalani showed him how to loop it between his legs.

"Hey, that's pretty comfortable," said John. "How do I look?"

Kalani laughed. "Like a pale fish swimming in the bay."

John shoved him and they fell to the floor, wrestling. The wrestling turned to tickling. Then they lay back, laughing.

At last John asked, "What do you know about these games? Surely they don't just play games all the time."

"I think we got here during the *Makahiki*," said Kalani. "Every year, the ancient Hawaiians went on a four-month vacation. Nobody worked. Nobody fought wars. Everybody had fun."

"And after the *Makahiki* was over?"

"Well, I guess then it was work as usual."

"I'm glad we came during vacation," said John.

"I hope we can find a way out before the *Makahiki* is over," said Kalani. "I don't remember too much of what I read, but I think life was hard back then... back... now?"

"It is confusing, isn't it?" giggled John. "Are we back then now? Or are we now back then?"

The two boys plopped onto their mats,

laughing. Then they pulled the other two mats over them for warmth and snuggled together, wondering what the next day would bring.

13. Makahiki Games

The next morning the big Hawaiian man came to their hut again. This time he wore Kalani's belt like a necklace, hanging loosely around his neck. He smiled and spoke to Kalani.

Kalani told John, "He says everyone must go to the contests today. We're too young to take part, but we can watch. I guess they're getting used to having us around."

They came to a clearing where young men were doing practice throws with spears and darts and stone disks. People watched along the edges of the field.

At last, two young men began to compete. First they threw long, heavy spears as far as they could. One man was clearly the stronger one. His spears went farther. Many people cheered.

Boys ran out to the field, collected the spears,

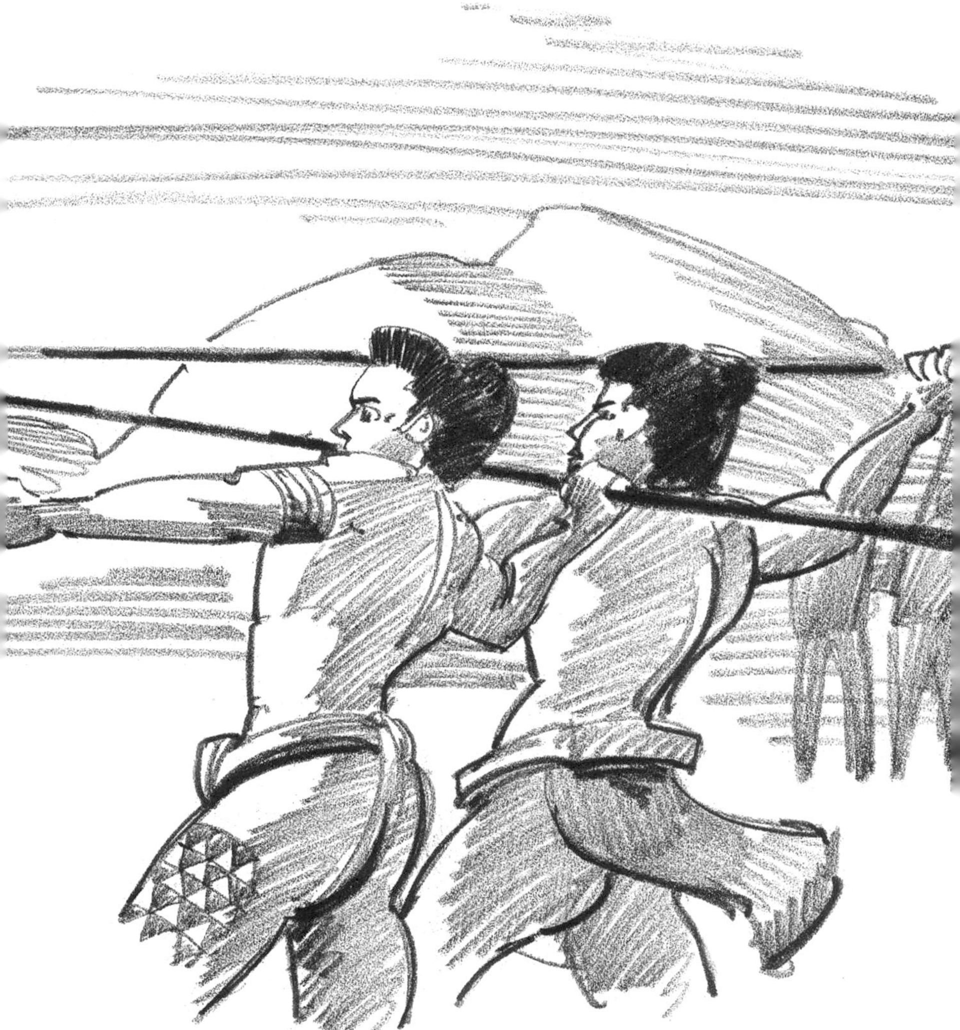

and brought them back to the two men. The men faced a new direction.

"Look," said Kalani. "There are stakes in the ground, close together, just like yesterday when the boys were playing."

This time, throwing straight was more important than throwing strong. The man who had won the distance throw stepped up to a mark. He sighted down the spear, raised his arm, and threw it with a sidewise motion. The spear zipped along the ground, straight between the two stakes.

The second man threw his spear. It also sped quickly between the stakes.

But when the first man threw again, his spear missed. When the second man's spear went cleanly between the stakes, everyone cheered. He was the winner of the second round.

Then the two rolled a stone disk. Again, the stronger man won on the distance. The second man won when rolling straight was important.

The contest was a tie.

Contests continued all day. Many men rolled the disk and threw the spears. Some shot bows and arrows at a target. Kalani and John walked around watching all the contests.

When evening came some of the people danced hula under a bright moon. Others slapped shiny gourds or clapped to the beat. It was mysterious and powerful.

Kalani explained. "They dance for the

Hawaiian gods, and they dance for each other. They have special schools where they train. I read that they study a long time, sometimes for years. They dance because they're happy, and to thank the gods for a good harvest."

The hula went on and on. Then the rhythm changed and the chanting grew louder.

"What are they saying?" whispered John.

"It's hard to understand," said Kalani. "Their language is a little different from the Hawaiian I know. But it's something about Kamehameha coming to O'ahu. It's something about a war."

"Kamehameha?" asked John.

"Yes. He's the one who stole the wooden statue, remember? The statue that helped people to win land. He's the one who captured Maui… and won the battle against the people on O'ahu."

Kalani thought about what he was saying. "Oh, no!" he said, putting his hand over his mouth.

"Kamehameha beat the people on O'ahu? Are we still on O'ahu?" asked John.

"Yes," Kalani nodded, his eyes dark with worry. "At least, I think we are."

The boys looked at each other. "Trouble ahead," said Kalani.

"Real trouble," agreed John.

14. What's A Hay-Yow?

The next morning Kalani woke up to see the big Hawaiian man in the doorway. "Time to go to work," the man told him. He wasn't wearing the belt; Kalani wondered where it was.

Makahiki was over.

After a quick breakfast, Kalani and John were marched down the path with the other older boys.

"Where are they taking us?" asked John.

"We're going to work on the *heiau*. Something about the floor," said Kalani.

"What's a hay-yow?" asked John.

"What's a *heiau*? Oh, I keep forgetting that you just came to Hawai'i. You don't know all this stuff. Well, do you remember that stone wall built in a square shape?"

"The one at the edge of the village?"

"Yes. That one. I think that's the *heiau*."

Kalani tripped over a root, then caught himself. He hurried to catch up to the boy in front of him.

"What's a *heiau* for?" asked John. He trotted to catch up to Kalani.

"Well, different ones were used for different things. Some were like boarding schools where young people learned special skills. At a fishing school *heiau*, they learned how to make fishhooks. Nets. Stuff like that. And they learned about the different kinds of fish and when people were allowed to catch them."

"What do you mean, allowed?" asked John, walking around a big rock in the path.

"The old-time Hawaiians had a good way to take care of the *'āina*, the land. If there weren't many fish, the king or the district chief would say they were *kapu*, taboo, not allowed. And everyone left the fish alone until the *kapu* was taken off. That way the fish could multiply."

"What happened if somebody caught fish that were *kapu*?"

Kalani didn't answer. He just kept walking.

"Come on, what happened? Tell me," John begged, grabbing Kalani by the shoulder.

Kalani half-turned toward John as he kept walking. "The people were killed," he whispered. "Killed right away, or killed in a *heiau*. That was what other *heiaus* were used for."

John asked, "How do you know if something's *kapu*? I sure don't want to end up like that, in a *heiau*."

"We'll just have to be very careful," said Kalani. "Do what the others do."

The man leading the group held up his hand. Everyone stopped. Then he started spacing them out along the trail. When they were an arm's length apart, they formed a long line. Men were joining them to work, too.

"Look," said Kalani. "Way down there. The ocean."

They could see shiny ripples far down the mountain, reflecting the sun's rays. It looked beautiful through the trees.

"What's going to happen now?" asked John.

"I don't know," said Kalani. "We just have to wait and find out."

A few minutes later, they knew.

A boy passed a smooth, flat rock to Kalani.

"Pass it on," said Kalani, handing it to John. "We're taking stream rocks up the mountain."

John gave the rock to the boy opposite him and turned back to Kalani to take another rock. And another.

"They're treating us like slaves," grumbled Kalani. "Who do they think they are?"

But he held his temper. He didn't dare complain to the leader. The leader carried a club. Kalani didn't want him to use it on him!

All morning long, the boys passed the smooth, flat rocks along the line.

At noon they broke for lunch. *Poi* again, and sweet potato, with water to drink.

They worked all afternoon. Kalani's arms ached. He had blisters on both hands from grabbing the rocks.

"I'm so tired," he whispered to John. "What about you?"

"I think my arms are going to fall off," John said. "When is this going to end?"

15. Blisters

That night they were allowed to go to the men's eating house for dinner. They didn't have to eat by themselves in the grass house.

"They must think we're one of them now," said Kalani. "I don't know if that's bad or good."

"Well," said John, "if I stay in the sun like this many more days, I'll kind of look like them. At least, I'll be as brown as they are."

After dinner the women and girls joined them around the fire. Kalani and the others watched and listened as one of the men made shapes with sennit string. As he stretched the string this way and that, he chanted a poem about the bird shape formed by the string. When he finished, he handed the string to Kalani. Kalani tried to twist and stretch it to make the shape of a bird, but the string got all tangled.

Laughing, the man straightened it out and

helped him try again.

Then another man asked a riddle. "Go through three walls to find water. What is it?"

Kalani translated for John. All the children thought and thought, but no one could guess the answer.

"A coconut!" the man said.

"Good one!" said Kalani, slapping his leg. "Clever, these old Hawaiians."

Back in their sleeping hut, Kalani was restless. His muscles ached from passing all those rocks. He and John both had broken blisters on their hands, and John had a fiery sunburn. Kalani could feel John's hot, restless body turning back and forth. He felt sorry for John, and he felt sorry for himself.

"You awake, John?" he asked.

"Yeah. My skin is itching so much, it's making me crazy. And it stings."

"Do you think we'll ever get back home?" asked Kalani.

"Home? You mean Honolulu? I sure hope so."

"I... I miss home. I miss Spotty," said Kalani. "I wonder if he's all right."

"Yes," said John. "And I could do with a plate of biscuits about now. And some bacon."

Kalani rolled over. "I wanted to go with Uncle Han to get the bamboo," he said.

"Yeah. And ride in the grocery wagon with Ruth. I bet you'd think that was fun too," said John.

Kalani punched John on the arm.

"Ow!" moaned John. "My sunburn! All right, I won't tease you about Ruth. But I'll bet that's one reason you want to go back."

"Maybe," admitted Kalani. "There's so much I want to do. I heard there's an elevator in the building that Uncle Han is working on downtown. I'd sure like to ride in it."

"How high is it?" asked John.

"Four stories, I think. High."

"Gee willikers! I'd like to ride in that, too."

"And telephones. Eddie said that Wong's Grocery is going to get a telephone," said Kalani. "You can talk to people clear across town with a telephone."

"Go on!" scoffed John.

"Yeah. Really." Kalani turned over and faced the doorway. "I never thought I'd miss the Wilsons. But right now I'd like to see them, too. And Chu Lee and Eddie and... and Ruth. But Lottie Jane—I'm sure glad I don't have to look at her pickle face."

He waited for John to reply, but all he heard was snoring. Kalani stared out into the night. He was miserable. The work was so hard. He wanted to go right out that door, to run away. *But what strange spirits are out there waiting for me?* he wondered. *And where would I go if I ran away?*

He scooted under the woven mat, hiding his head.

At last, he too fell asleep.

The next day they worked on the rock line again, passing stone after stone up the mountain. Their broken blisters formed new blisters underneath, but not as big as the ones formed the day before. Their hands became calloused and they didn't hurt so much.

Lunch was a treat. Birds had been killed that morning, gutted and stuffed with long, thin, hot stones. By lunchtime, the hot stones had cooked the birds from the inside out. Each person had a few bites. It was delicious with *poi*.

Late in the afternoon the leader told them they could go back to the village.

"I'd like to get a better look at that *heiau*," said Kalani. "We're doing all this work to fix it up. I want to know what they're doing with these flat stones."

"Let's try to sneak over there on our way back home," said John.

The boys walked slowly, letting the others pass them on purpose. They were the last ones to reach the village.

They slipped down the shadowy path toward the *heiau*.

"Look, there's a pile of stones inside the *heiau*," said Kalani. "I think those are the ones we've been passing along."

"Looks like it," said John. "They're placing them all over the ground."

"Ah," said Kalani. "Then the floor won't be muddy when it rains."

"There's another walled-off place with higher walls."

"I wonder what that's for," said Kalani. "It's like a little room inside the *heiau*, but there's no door to get inside."

"Yeah. Funny," said John.

Before long, John would find out what the little room was for. And he wouldn't think it was funny. Not funny at all.

16. Honor The King!

The next morning Kalani and John were wakened early.

"I wonder where they are taking us," Kalani said. "This is a different path."

All the boys and some of the men walked single file down the path. They were taken down to level ground near the ocean to work in the taro field. Standing in water up to their ankles, they planted the taro in long rows. Kalani remembered how he loved to squish mud through his fingers when he was little. But this was different. This was work. Backbreaking work.

Suddenly, Kalani heard the moan of a conch shell. The leader shouted, "Down! The chief is coming!"

Immediately, each person fell face down in the water. Kalani held very still. He didn't dare move. He knew if the chief saw him looking at him, he might be killed. He held his breath as long as he could. Then he blew bubbles in the water. At last, he raised his nose up just enough to breathe.

Not a moment too soon, the leader said, "All right, the chief is gone now. Back to work." Everyone got up. The chief was out of sight.

Kalani looked at John. "Wow, John, you need a bath! You look like a mud man."

John looked strange. He was covered with mud from head to foot except for his round eyes. The dark mud made his eyes seem as white as two pigeons in the moonlight.

"Same as you," said John, flicking some muddy water off his arm into Kalani's face. "You won't take any beauty prize, either. You look like a pig that's been rooting in a mud puddle! But maybe this mud will help my sunburn," he added, patting his cheek.

"All right," barked the leader in Hawaiian. "Back to work. Stop playing." Kalani didn't need to tell John what he said. The tone of his voice said it all.

Kalani bent over to work again, mud dripping down into the water from his arms and stomach.

Finally they were given a break. Everyone ran to the shore and dove into the cool blue salty ocean. Kalani scrubbed the mud from his tired body, splashing and ducking under the water.

At first the salt water stung his sore hands.

Then it began to heal them.

The boys let the waves lift them and float them to shore. Then they dove through the waves to play some more, sputtering as the salty water filled their noses.

Kalani dove under John's legs and lifted him onto his shoulders. John dove into the water from Kalani's shoulders. The other boys copied them, laughing at the new game.

A man came paddling a canoe to shore. He talked with the leader, waving his hands and pointing toward the east. Then he got back in his canoe and paddled on.

"I wonder what that was all about," said John.

"I don't know," said Kalani, "but the leader looks kind of worried."

Sitting on dry land at lunchtime, Kalani thought about the man in the canoe and about the chief who had walked by without warning. When it was *Makahiki* time, everyone was happy and relaxed. Now there was a feeling of fear, a feeling of danger in the air.

He told John, "Be very careful around chiefs and kings. Don't even let your shadow come near them. Their guards would take you away. They might kill you. You wouldn't even have time to say you were sorry."

"They don't give you a trial, or anything?" asked John, setting down the piece of sweet potato he had been nibbling.

"No," said Kalani. "If a chief or a king says to kill you, then you're dead."

Suddenly a man came trotting along the path. "Make way, make way," the man shouted. He carried a pole across his shoulder with a huge gourd hanging from each end.

Everyone fell face down on the ground. Everyone except John. He just sat looking at the man with the gourds.

"Seize him," the leader of the work group said. "He has dishonored the king's drinking water."

"What?" said John. "Drinking water? What are you talking about?"

But before he could say anything more, strong arms carried him up the mountain. Toward the *heiau*.

Kalani watched him go, keeping his tears and fear inside. He had warned John about chiefs and kings. He hadn't warned him about the things that were needed for royalty. Things such as pure drinking water carried from high up the stream. He felt guilty. He felt it was his fault that John was carried off.

17. The Rescue

Kalani had no appetite that night. He worried about John. Was he still alive?

Sitting by the fire, Kalani listened to the talk around him. The man who had been their leader at the taro field asked a riddle. "Blood before. Blood after. Thunder in the middle."

No one could figure it out. Kalani felt the skin on the back of his neck tighten. This didn't sound like the joking kind of riddle people had told on other nights.

The man who had asked the riddle looked serious. "It's about Kamehameha," he said. "When we were at the taro field today, while we were playing in the ocean, a man paddled in with a message. Kamehameha has conquered Maui. Now he is heading here to O'ahu."

"Oh, no," a young woman whimpered. She

began to moan.

"And the riddle?" another woman asked. "Explain the riddle."

The man paused a moment, staring into the fire.

"Blood before. The priests will have to sacrifice many people. Perhaps that will convince the war god to protect us."

Another man spoke up. "I think that brown-haired speckle-faced boy will be the first one the priest will choose."

"Yes," the other people murmured in agreement.

"He has already broken a *kapu*," said one old woman.

Kalani shuddered.

"Thunder in the middle," continued the old woman. "That would be the battle."

"Yes," said the man who told the riddle. "And blood after. We don't know whose blood. Maybe the blood of Kamehameha's warriors. Maybe ours."

"Or maybe both," Kalani muttered, trying to remember everything he'd read about the great battle. History had bored him—it seemed to be all dates and kings and battles—he had only read the history book because Teacher made him.

He looked at the people sitting around the fire, some worried, some scared, some defiant. A man put a sheltering arm around his wife. A woman shushed her baby, rocking it in her arms, her eyes wide with fear.

Kalani remembered from his studies that Kamehameha would be the victor. Kamehameha had a strong army, and he had guns from the English sailors. But which of these people would die and which would live? The history book hadn't said anything about the ordinary people.

Silently, families stood up and walked to their sleeping huts, hoping to get a little rest before the coming battle.

Kalani was tired from working in the taro field. His back ached from bending over all day, but he wasn't sleepy. He was worried about John. And he was worried about the coming of Kamehameha.

I wonder how long they will keep John alive in the heiau, he thought. I wonder how many others they will sacrifice. And how will they choose them? Will they take me, too?

From another hut, Kalani heard a baby crying.

I wish I could go back to the Wilsons, he thought. Odd. I never thought I would get homesick for a crying baby.

Kalani began to plot his escape. He had to get out of there.

If I can find that lava tube, maybe I can get back to the Wilsons. But... I can't go back without John. I have to get him out of the heiau.

Kalani looked outside. The fires were dead. It was so dark he could barely see the next hut.

I can't go out there, he thought. *The only time I went out in the dark, the Night Marchers kidnapped me.*

He stood at the doorway, trying to see any ghosts that might be waiting for him. He wanted to rescue John. He wanted to make his feet walk up that path to the *heiau.* But his legs would not move. They were frozen stiff from fear.

His stomach began to twist inside. He was so scared! So worried! The pain made him double over.

He sat down, facing the door. *I can't go out there. I can't do it.*

He squeezed his arms against his stomach, trying to make it stop hurting. The baby in the other hut began to fuss again. Kalani thought about the Wilsons, about John, about Kamehameha and the sacrifices.

"Ghosts or no ghosts, I have to do it," he scolded himself.

Kalani stood up and forced himself to walk out the door into the dark. Trembling, he crept slowly up the path through the dark toward the *heiau.* No one saw him. Not even the ghosts.

18. Up The Mountain

He reached the outside wall of the *heiau*, happy to feel the rough stones at last.

"John? Are you in there?" he whispered.

There was no answer.

"John," he said, a little louder. "Did they bring you here?"

"Yes." John's voice came from the little room inside the *heiau*. "I'm in here. But I think there's a guard outside. Be quiet."

Kalani clambered over the low wall of the *heiau*. He bent down so no one could see him, rushed to the higher wall inside, and gazed all around. He didn't see a guard.

He climbed up the higher wall and peered down. In the dark, he could faintly see John standing in the little room, looking up at him.

"Help me," John whispered. "The insides of

the walls are so slick, I can't climb out."

Kalani reached down as far as he could. John stretched up. Their fingertips barely touched.

"Jump," whispered Kalani. "Grab my wrists."

John jumped. Not high enough.

He jumped again and grabbed hold of Kalani's wrists. He planted his feet against the wall.

Kalani stretched and stretched. His arms felt like they were being pulled off. The rough stones of the walled room scraped his bare chest.

He pulled John up the wall. John swung his legs over. They jumped down and landed on the floor of the *heiau*.

Kalani bent over and raced to the outside wall. John followed. Quickly, they searched for a guard. They didn't see anyone.

They scrambled over the low wall and disappeared into the forest.

"Don't look back," said Kalani. "Just run!"

They could hardly see the path, but they sped on. Kalani pulled John along, stumbling over tree roots and rocks, falling, getting up, then racing even faster.

Far behind them, Kalani heard voices shouting.

"I think they know we're gone," John said.

Kalani stopped, doubling over with pain. "I can't run any more," he panted. He shoved his hand into his side, trying to stop the stitch. "My side..."

It was dangerous to stop. But Kalani's side hurt so much he couldn't move.

"We have to run," said John. "Even if your side does hurt."

He grabbed Kalani's hand and dragged him along the path. They pushed on, up the mountainside. Every time Kalani tried to stop, John dragged him on.

"Look for a cave," said Kalani. "Or anywhere to hide."

Below them, they saw torches. People were hunting for them.

Kalani said, "I don't know if those are real people or Night Marchers. But I know they're after us. We've got to find somewhere to hide. And quick!"

"Under these bushes," said John. "Don't move. Don't talk."

The boys lay flat on the ground under the bushes. Kalani forced himself to keep his face down. He wanted to look up to see where the searchers were going. But he didn't let himself. The searchers must not see the whites of his eyes. That would give him away as surely as a torchlight.

As the searchers rushed by, the boys could hear footsteps with the voices.

Footsteps.

So these are real people, not Night Marchers, thought Kalani. Somehow, that didn't make him feel much better.

The pain in his side was gone, but his stomach ache came back. It felt like there was a rat inside his body, trying to gnaw its way out. He crossed his arms over his stomach and hugged himself, but the terrible pain would not go away.

Finally, there were no footsteps, no voices. Kalani pushed himself up, forgetting the pain.

John glanced around. "Kalani, look behind us. Back through the bushes."

A cave!

19. Watching Kamehameha

Kalani led the way, crawling into the cave.

"It's so dark," whispered John. "I can't see anything. What if snakes are in here?"

"No snakes," said Kalani, still clutching his stomach. "We don't have snakes in Hawai'i." He didn't tell John there might be scorpions or centipedes or spiders... or ghosts.

As his eyes adjusted to the darkness, Kalani saw that the passage widened and became higher ahead. He stood up and took a deep breath. "I think we need to feel our way through this lava tube," he said. "We don't want to stay near the entrance. When daylight comes we could see a little better at the cave entrance, but so could those people who are searching for us."

"Okay," said John, stumbling to his feet. "I'll follow you."

The boys began to feel their way, dragging their fingers along the damp, musty-smelling wall. They couldn't tell how far they went or how long they travelled, but to Kalani it seemed they walked for hours.

Kalani still felt like a rat was gnawing the inside of his stomach. Now and then the pain stabbed so sharply it took his breath away. He wondered if he was sick. Lottie Jane had an attack of appendicitis once, and the doctor had to operate. The doctor said he had gotten it just in time—whatever that meant. Kalani worried that his stomach ache was appendicitis, too. But there was no doctor to help him here in this cave.

He walked on, feeling his way in the dark. Finally, they came to the end of the lava tube and looked out. They could barely see the valley in the dim starlight.

"What a beautiful valley," said John.

"I think it's Nu'uanu Valley, where Uncle Han gets his bamboo," said Kalani.

He stood up straight and looked over the dark valley. He took a deep breath.

He thought, *I made myself go out in the darkness. And I helped John escape from the heiau. And now, we've come through the lava tube and left the searchers behind.*

He was pleased with himself. He rubbed his stomach, then smiled. Now that he wasn't afraid, the pain started to go away. Maybe the pain wasn't from appendicitis after all. Maybe it was just from fear.

He said, "Yes, I'm sure this is Nu'uanu Valley. I wonder which century we are in."

"I don't know. Let's wait for daylight," said John. "What is this tunnel, anyway?"

"It's made by a volcano," said Kalani. "Teacher told us about lava tubes. When a volcano erupts, the lava cools faster on top. The hot lava underneath keeps flowing. When the volcano quiets down, the hot lava keeps spilling out the end of the tube and makes a hollow tunnel."

"Wow. We didn't have anything like that in Boston," said John, patting the wall of the tunnel.

Kalani sat down at the mouth of the cave and John lay on his stomach beside him, looking out over the valley. The boys were quiet for a while, listening to the birds twittering in the trees below, waiting for the dawn.

"I'll be glad to get back to the Wilsons," said John. "I don't mind telling you, when I was stuck in that *heiau*, I was scared. I thought I'd never see the Wilsons again."

"I'll be glad to see them, too," said Kalani. "And after the way we worked in that village, the chores at the Wilsons will seem easy as pie. But I don't know about..."

"What? You sound like you don't really want to go back," John said.

"Oh, I want to go back all right. But that

bawling baby, I wish she'd... I just wish they'd give her away, or..."

"Maybe we can find out why she cries so much," said John.

"Yeah. Maybe so."

The sky began to turn a little pink. Distant cries came up the valley. The sound of a gun. The shouts of men. Echoing back and forth between the valley walls.

"What's going on?" asked Kalani.

"It sounds like a battle," said John.

The boys looked to the west, away from the sunrise. Hundreds of men were coming up the valley floor, fighting. Some threw spears or shot arrows. Some swung war clubs covered with dog's teeth.

"Look at that!" said John. "It's two armies. And they're dressed in the old-time style."

"And with old-time weapons," said Kalani. "Except for those few with guns. This *is* Nuʻuanu Valley..."

"What about it?" asked John. "You look worried."

"Nuʻuanu Valley is where Kamehameha fought the last big battle on Oʻahu. The armies fought all the way to the Pali, over there where the sun's rising. The warriors on the losing side—the ones who were still alive—went over the cliff."

"My gosh! What a battle!" said John. "Well, it looks like we are sitting in the front row, watching history."

"I think you're right. Don't move. Don't make a sound. We don't want them to come up here after us."

All day the boys watched the men fight in the valley far below. They were so spellbound they didn't even get hungry.

Finally, the warriors fought on up the valley, away from the cave where the boys were hiding. The woods grew quiet.

"What do you think?" asked Kalani. "Should we go down?"

"No. It wouldn't do any good," said John. "This is still the wrong century. I think we have to find the cave entrance where we came in. The place up above the Wilson's house."

"I think you're right," said Kalani. "Sometimes lava tubes branch off into other passages. Let's see what we can find."

They started back into the tube. After a short distance, it was dark. Daytime was as dark as nighttime in the tubes. Kalani's heart beat fast.

Darkness! Spirits might be in darkness.

A sharp pain stabbed his stomach. Then he remembered. He didn't have to be afraid of the dark anymore. He had ventured out in the dark village to rescue John. He had felt his way in the dark lava tube last night. Now he knew he was stronger than the darkness.

The pain began to go away.

Kalani inched along, blindly touching the sides of the lava tube with his fingertips.

"Shhh," he said at last, putting his hand back to stop John. "Don't move. I hear something."

Kalani held his breath. In the distance he could hear a noise.

"What is it?" whispered John.

"I think it's a dog," said Kalani. "Maybe it's Spotty!"

But if it wasn't Spotty, could it be a Night Marcher? Or an old-time warrior?

Kalani screwed up his courage and shouted. "Spotty! Here Spotty!"

20. Tummy Aches

They could hear the click-click-clicking of a little dog's toenails on the lava tube floor. Suddenly the dog leaped on Kalani's chest, pushing him backward.

Then the dog ran away, barking. Sure enough, it was Spotty, leading them home!

The boys chased after him, following his bark. Out of the dark cave. Into the blinding sunlight. Down the beautiful green mountain. Along the dirt streets. All the way home. The Wilson house with its white board fence looked wonderful.

Mama was standing on the *lānai*, wiping her hands on her apron.

"My goodness, boys! Where have you been? The whole neighborhood is out looking for you. I don't know whether to spank you or hug you."

She gave Kalani a hug, and then hugged John.

"Oh, boys, I was so worried about you!" She hugged them again, both at the same time. "I'm so glad you're back. Chu Lee, he will be so happy. He was out with the search party most of the night. And Lottie Jane, well I thought she'd cry her eyes out worrying about you, poor thing."

"Lottie Jane?" asked Kalani, thinking he hadn't heard right. "Lottie Jane? Worrying about me?"

"Yes. You don't understand that one. Underneath all that sass there's a real soft heart, I tell you," said Mama.

Then she stood back and looked them over. "Just look at you. Dressed in *malos*, covered with dirt. Have you been play-acting somewhere?"

"No, ma'am. Yes, ma'am." said John. "I don't really know how to explain it."

"Well, let's get you cleaned up and into some fresh clothes. I'll bet you haven't had breakfast either."

"No ma'am," said Kalani. Suddenly his stomach felt hollow. "Breakfast would be great."

Then Kalani heard the baby crying inside the house.

"The baby. Still fussing," said Kalani.

"Yes," said Mama. "But we got us a hired girl to help care for her. I need to have more time for you other *keiki*. I shouldn't be taking care of her all the time."

Kalani grinned at John. Maybe things would work out after all.

The boys went inside and took turns at the pump in the sink. Mama brought in some fresh clothes. "I found your belt this morning, Kalani," she said. "It was outside in the yard."

The hair on the back of Kalani's neck stood up and he got chicken skin all down his arms. But he didn't offer an explanation—he couldn't explain something he didn't understand.

"Yes, Mama," he said, as he continued washing up.

Still the baby cried.

Kalani asked, "What do you suppose is wrong with her?"

"Some babies just cry," said Mama. "The doctor said it was colic. He said she would outgrow it."

Kalani looked closely at Mama. For the first time, he saw how tired she was. The lines in her face, the puffiness under her eyes, the slump of her body. Why hadn't he seen it before?

"I guess you get pretty tired, taking care of her," he said.

"Oh, Kalani, you have no idea. I'm worn out, that's the truth. Nights when she cries and cries and cries, I feel like crying right along with her."

Mama wiped her eyes with her apron. "I feel so sorry for her. That tummy ache, it just won't go away."

Kalani's eyes grew big. Stomach aches were powerfully painful.

"You think she has a tummy ache?" he asked.

"Yes. That's what colic is," said Mama, walking to the woodbox. She pulled out a stick of wood, turned the handle on the front of the iron cookstove, and shoved the stick inside, poking up the fire.

Kalani thought, If she's got a *tummy* ache, *no wonder she cries all the time!*

21. All The Same Family

Kalani and John finished washing. They took turns with the towel, drying their hands and arms, and hung the towel on a nail.

Kalani asked, "What's her name, that baby? I don't remember."

Mama started scrambling eggs and slicing bread. She looked pleased that he was interested in the baby.

"It's Mary Elizabeth," she said. "We just call her Beth. That's a long enough name for such a tiny baby."

She set two bowls of oatmeal on the table with a pitcher of milk. "Eat your cereal. The eggs are almost ready."

The boys gobbled their food, forgetting their table manners. For once, Mama didn't correct them.

"Where were you boys? Where did you spend the night?" she asked again. She dished scrambled eggs onto their plates, then cut thick slices of bread to go with them.

Kalani raised his eyebrows and shook his head at John. Then he grinned. "We, uh... we got lost."

Kalani knew better than to talk about Night Marchers and ancient Hawaiians. He'd seen Lottie Jane get whipped for telling tall tales. He knew what would happen to him if he told Mama the real story.

"And we spent the night in a cave, a lava tube," added John.

"Well, I'm glad Spotty found you," Mama said. "You gave us all a scare, yeah?"

"Were we gone just one night?" asked Kalani.

"Yes. What did you think?"

"It seemed longer," said Kalani. "Lots longer."

"I guess when you're lost it can seem like a very long time," she said.

Mama began to clear away the dishes, stacking them in a metal dishpan in the sink. "It's too late for you to go to school today," she said, "but the vegetable garden can use some weeding."

Kalani grinned at John. "Easy enough, yeah John?"

Mama gave Kalani a funny look. "Kalani, I never knew you to do chores without a complaint or two. I'd sure like to know where you boys have been. You seem so different."

The baby continued to cry.

"I better go show the hired girl how to take care of Beth," Mama said, patting the boys' shoulders.

Kalani didn't mind any more if Mrs. Wilson couldn't give him a lot of attention. He just felt sorry for little Beth with her stomach ache. He shuddered, remembering his own pain the night before.

"I wish I could help that baby," said Kalani.

John said, "I stayed with the Wong's when I first came to Hawai'i. When Ruth's little sister had a tummy ache, they gave her some ginger tea. That stuff settled her right down."

"Hmmm. Maybe that would work for our baby," Kalani said. Then he caught himself. "I mean, the Wilson's baby." His face turned red.

"I guess it's okay to call her 'our baby,'" said John. "After all, she's part of the family."

"Yes," said Kalani. "You're right. We're all the same family."

He pushed his chair back from the table. "Let's get our chores done, John. I want to take the trolley to Wong's Grocery. Maybe we can buy some ginger. After all, I am the oldest boy. I ought to take some responsibility for little Beth."

"And maybe you can see Ruth while we're there," teased John.

Kalani punched him in the arm. But not very

hard.

"And maybe we can tell Ruth and Eddie about what happened to us," added John. "How we lived in that ancient village, and how we saw Kamehameha and the soldiers fighting."

"And maybe not," said Kalani, shaking his head. "I'm sure no one will ever believe us."

THE END

You Can Bowl Ancient Hawaiian Style

A popular game among children and adults in Old Hawai'i was similar to bowling.

If you want to play outside, place two rocks about six inches apart. Stand back about five feet. Slide a flat, narrow rock between them. If you can slide it through without touching either boundary rock, you get a point. For your next turn, move back a step.

The person with the most points wins.

If you want to play inside, play on a vinyl or wooden floor. You can use cans of soda or books as boundaries and also as the slider, or anything that is fairly heavy and longer than it is wide.

The same rules apply as in the outside version.

The games the ancient Hawaiians played were fun, but most of them also improved their fighting skills.

Orphans

Many people lived short lives in the 1800s. In fact, it was somewhat unusual for a fifteen-year-old person to have both parents still alive!

Many people died from disease. This was before antibiotics and vaccines were discovered. It was before refrigerators: food spoiled easily, causing food poisoning. And people didn't know that eating fruits and vegetables could help prevent some diseases.

The cholera that killed Kalani's family spread because there was no sewer system in Honolulu at that time.

People also died through accidents and violence. So there were a lot of children without parents. In Hawai'i, there were many homes such as the Wilsons, with orphans of different ethnic backgrounds living together like brothers and sisters.

Even now in Hawai'i, we have the custom of *hānai*: a child goes to live with another family and becomes "their child," although no formal adoption papers are signed. Sometimes the *hānai* family is related to the child. Sometimes they are just friends.

In Case You're Wondering

We think Hawaiians came during two different periods, probably sailing north from the Marquesas and Society Islands. We don't know if they explored for adventure or if they were forced out of their original homeland by overpopulation (too many people for the amount of farmland, causing food shortages). Or perhaps they angered a powerful person and were banished.

Some scientists believe they got the idea from the migrating birds, especially the *kōlea*, or plover, which left every spring and came back every fall, proving there had to be land to the north.

These early explorers sailed over a vast expanse of ocean, navigating by the stars, wind, smells, floating vegetation, and ocean currents. There is some evidence that they maintained contact with other island peoples, traveling back and forth.

The first period of settlement was probably around the eighth century. This group seems to have been rather peaceful. The second period of settlement probably was in the eleventh to fourteenth centuries. Anthropologists believe that the priests in this second group made cruel laws and often demanded human sacrifice.

Kamehameha conquered all the islands

except Kaua'i through warfare; he won control of Kaua'i by tricking its chieftain. Europeans began to arrive in the Hawaiian Islands shortly before the battle in Nu'uanu Valley. The guns Kamehameha bought from the Europeans probably helped more in winning the battle than the statue made from the breadfruit tree.

Before the Europeans and Americans arrived, Hawaiians cared for the *'āina*, the land. They knew how to keep the soil fertile and the seas abundant with fish.

Although some warriors fought frequent battles and used vicious weapons, many people lived quietly. They farmed and fished, made *tapa* cloth, wove baskets, and played in the ocean. Each year everyone in all the Hawaiian Islands enjoyed a four-month time of peace and recreation during *Makahiki.*

THE END, REALLY AND TRULY

Glossary

'āina   land, earth

ali'i   chief, chiefess, royalty

hānai   foster or adopted child

haole   white person

heiau   place of worship, shrine

kapu   taboo, forbidden

keiki   child

kōlea   Pacific golden plover, a migratory bird

lānai   porch

Makahiki   ancient festival, now replaced by Aloha Week

malo   loincloth

pili   grass used to thatch houses

poi   cooked taro; also, slang for a mixed breed animal

ti   tropical plant with many uses

tutu   grandmother